THE SANTA THIEF

Written by **Alane Adams**
Illustrated by **Lauren Gallegos**

spark press

SparkPress
80 E. Rio Salado Pkwy, Suite 511
Tempe, AZ 85281
www.gosparkpress.com

Printed in the United States of America

Library of Congress Cataloging-in-Publication Data
Adams, Alane.
The Santa Thief / Alane Adams; Illustrated by Lauren Gallegos. — 1st ed.
p. cm.
ISBN 978-1-940716-86-2
1. The main category of the book —History —Other category. 2. Another subject category —From one perspective. 3. More categories —And their modifiers. I. Johnson, Ben. II. Title.
HF0000.A0 A00 2010
299.000 00–dc22 2010999999

First Edition
Cover and book design by Lauren Gallegos

For Baby Kason —A.A.

For Grandpa Manuel —L.G.

Christmas, 1929

The day was bright and sunny as Georgie followed Papa into the woods. A fresh blanket of snow covered the ground. Georgie's feet were cold, but he didn't mind.

Tomorrow was Christmas, which meant today was the day they picked out their tree.

Georgie hurried to keep up. "Do you think Santa got my letter about the new skates?" he asked.

The pond was frozen over, and Georgie wanted to go skating, but his old skates were too small.

"I don't know, Georgie. Santa has a lot on his mind." Papa came to a stop in front of a tree. "How about this one?"

Georgie craned his head back, studying it. "It's too tall." He looked at Papa. "But Santa won't forget, right?"

Papa just shrugged and kept walking deeper into the woods. "Do you like this one?"

Georgie spread his arms out. "Too wide." He couldn't stop thinking about those new skates. "Papa, I've been very good this year. I do all my chores and I get good marks in school. So, do you think he'll bring me skates?"

Papa patted his shoulder. "I don't know if Santa's coming this year, Georgie. Times have been tough, even for Santa. Maybe next year."

Georgie sagged. Next year was too long to wait.

Papa marched on and then came to a stop. "Well? How about this one?"

It was a nice tree. Not too wide. Not too tall. The branches were full and springy. But Georgie wasn't excited anymore. If Santa wasn't coming, what was the point of a Christmas tree?

"I guess so," he mumbled.

They dragged the tree back to
Papa's truck.

"Oh no!" Papa said, patting his pockets.

"What's wrong, Papa?"

"My key fell out of my pocket. It could
take hours to find, and I have an important
stop to make before the shops close."

But luckily, Georgie spied something
shiny in the snow. "It's right here, Papa.
It must have fallen out when you loaded
the tree."

They pulled up in front of Ray's Hardware Store. There in the window was a pair of shiny silver skates. Georgie put his hands on the glass, dreaming of flying across the ice.

"Hey, Georgie." His friend Harley walked up. "The boys and I'll be out on Sparrow Pond after supper tomorrow. You coming?"

Georgie looked away from the skates and shook his head. "No. My skates are too small."

"Too bad for you," Harley said.

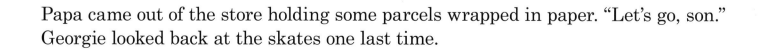

Papa came out of the store holding some parcels wrapped in paper. "Let's go, son."
Georgie looked back at the skates one last time.

Back home, Mama was waiting
with the box of decorations.
"Do you want to put the first
ornament on, Georgie?"

"No, you go ahead."

Mama frowned. "What on earth's gotten into you?"

"Nothing." Georgie scuffed the floor with the toe of his boot.

Mama set the box down and knelt before him. "Georgie, this isn't like you. You love to help me decorate the tree."

"Papa says Santa's not bringing me skates this year," Georgie burst out. "So Christmas is ruined."

"Christmas isn't about the gifts," Mama scolded. "It's about doing something special for others. Why don't you go to your room and think about that?"

Georgie dragged himself off and lay down on his bed. He really, really wanted those skates. Buster came in holding an ornament in his mouth. He dropped it in Georgie's hand. The round face was painted like Santa's. It gave Georgie an idea. "Buster, you're a genius!"

Georgie cracked open the door
to his room. Mama and Papa
were busy decorating the tree.

He snuck across the hall into
their room. Mama's sewing kit
was on the dresser.

In the closet, he found a pair of Papa's long johns. He took one of Papa's belts, a pair of old boots, and a few other things, and took them back to his room.

At supper, Mama asked if anyone had seen her sewing kit, but Georgie said nothing. He ate fast and hurried back to his room.

Georgie worked late into the night,

sewing and gluing

and making his gifts.

When morning came, Georgie was ready. He tightened Papa's belt, put on his black boots, and clomped into the living room. Mama and Papa were sitting in front of the tree.

"Ho ho ho," Georgie said in a deep voice. "Merry Christmas."
They looked up in surprise. "Is that Santa Claus?"
Mama said with a smile.

Georgie nodded. His face was
hidden behind a white beard made
of cotton. He had Papa's long johns belted
around his waist, and a pillow stuffed in
his shirt for extra padding. He had even
made a red Santa hat!

"I've got gifts for you," Georgie said. He handed Mama a box.

Mama looked surprised. "What on earth?" She quickly opened it.

"Look, Papa, Santa made me a new pincushion."

"Your old one had holes in it. Now you, Papa." Georgie handed Papa his gift.

"Santa hasn't brought me something in years," Papa said gruffly. He opened the box and smiled. "Santa made me a keychain. Now I won't lose my key. What a wonderful Christmas! Thank you, Santa!"

Georgie took off his beard. "It's me, Papa. Isn't this the best Christmas ever?"

"It is," Papa agreed.

"Hmm, Georgie, is that a box under the tree?" Mama asked.
Georgie got on his knees and reached under the branches.
His fingers touched something hard.
"I feel it," he said. "What is it?"
"You'll have to open it and see," Mama said.
Georgie dragged the box out and tore the paper off.
His eyes grew wide.

"I thought Santa wasn't coming this year," he said, lifting up the pair of new skates.

"Those are from us," Papa said. "I worked extra shifts, and Mama baked pies and sold them."

"Merry Christmas, Georgie," Mama said, holding her arms out.

Georgie threw his arms around her. "Merry Christmas, Mama."